Mystery

of the

Tooth Gremlin

By the same author

The Best, Worst Day

Mystery
of the
Tooth Gremlin

Bonnie Graves

Illustrated by **Paige Billin-Frye**

Hyperion Books for Children
New York

To Erin—who knows that reading books *does* get
you places—for your help with this one and your
unwavering faith in all the others
—B. G.

Text © 1997 by Bonnie Graves.
Illustrations © 1997 by Paige Billin-Frye.

Printed in the United States of America.

First Edition

1 3 5 7 9 10 8 6 4 2

The artwork for each picture is prepared using pen and ink.
This book is set in 16-point Berkeley Book.

Library of Congress Cataloging-in-Publication Data

Graves, Bonnie B.
Mystery of the Tooth Gremlin / Bonnie Graves ;
illustrated by Paige Billin-Frye. — 1st ed.
p. cm.
Summary: Although he wants to track down the Tooth Gremlin, Jesse has to read three
books by Friday, or his class cannot go on a field trip.
ISBN 0-7868-1158-7 (pbk.) — ISBN 0-7868-2238-4 (lib. bdg.)
[1. Teeth—Fiction. 2. Reading—Fiction. 3. Schools—Fiction.
4. Mystery and detective stories.] I. Billin-Frye, Paige, ill.
II. Title.
PZ7. G77515My 1997
[E]—dc20 96-26832

Table of Contents

1
Uh-Oh!

"Jesse Stone," Ms. Noori said. "Come up to my desk, please."

Uh-oh. He knew what she was going to ask. *Book reports.* She asked it every morning. What would he tell her this time?

Jesse looked over at his best buddies, Bip and Will. They shrugged. Did they have their book reports done? He wiggled his loose tooth with his tongue.

1

As Jesse hopped up to his teacher's desk, Maxine Macmillan, the smartest kid in Blue Unit, glared at him. Why? he wondered. Maybe he had hopped on her toe. But he sure hadn't felt anything.

When he reached Ms. Noori's desk and saw the look on his teacher's face, something strange happened. Words just sort of flew out

2

of Jesse's mouth before he could stop them. He didn't know where they came from. "I have a book report today." *Uh-oh.*

Ms. Noori's eyebrows went up, and her eyes got as big and round as Tootsie Pops. "Jesse, that's super! Then all you need to read is two more. Remember you said you'd read three books?"

"I did?"

"Yeah, you did," said Lyddie. She stood beside Ms. Noori's desk, waiting to take the lunch money to the office. "*Three* book reports."

Ms. Noori reached into her desk for the lunch-money envelope but kept her eyes on Jesse. "Blue Unit needs one hundred books read by Friday, you know, to earn that trip to the police station to see Detective Kelly," she reminded him. Ms. Noori had the idea that reading books was the way to get places. Every time they planned a trip somewhere she made them read books.

Jesse looked up at the Book Report Chart, then at the Lost Tooth Chart. His name was on neither. But that was going to change. Soon. Jesse's tongue found his loose tooth, which was now hanging by just a thread. Jesse felt a little flutter in his stomach when he thought about seeing his name on the chart and imagined a shark's tooth in his pocket, the one his dad had promised to bring him from Hawaii.

"Look," he said. He grinned and pushed his front tooth forward with his tongue so

Ms. Noori could see how loose it was. "I'm getting a real shark's tooth for this one when my parents come back from Hawaii."

Lyddie blew air out through her teeth. She sounded like a snake and looked like one, too. "Big deal," she said as she grabbed the brown lunch-money envelope.

Ms. Noori frowned at Lyddie, but then

she smiled at Jesse. "That's wonderful, Jesse. But don't forget book reports. You don't want to keep the class from going to the police station, do you?"

Jesse shook his head. He hoped Ms. Noori wouldn't call his reading group first today. That would give him time to read a book.

As he hopped back to his desk, Maxine sat staring at the charts. She still looked mad. But why? She had ten books next to her name on the Book Report Chart and drawings of six teeth by her name on the Lost Tooth Chart. If anyone should be happy, it should be Maxine.

Back at his desk, Jesse's tongue found his loose tooth once again and pushed hard, harder, and hardest. *Snap!* His tooth was free at last!

He plucked the tooth from his mouth. It was a little bloody, so he wiped it on his sleeve, then held it out to admire. Wow! The most beautiful tooth he had ever seen, so white and shiny, almost like a pearl—a pearl from Hawaii!

Next he pulled a baseball card from his collection. His best. Hernando Hernandez.

He set the card on the corner of his desk, then placed the tooth right on top of Hernando. Ms. Noori had a special box for teeth, but Jesse wanted to look at his for a while. After all, it was his very first tooth.

Every other kid in Blue Unit had lost at least two, even the first graders. One third grader had lost a dozen! Jesse was in second grade and still had all his baby teeth. Every

single one of them . . . until now. But this tooth was going to earn him a shark's tooth. Some things were worth waiting for.

While Jesse sat admiring his tooth, he heard Ms. Noori call his reading group.

"Super Turtles," she announced.

Uh-oh! Book report time. What was he going to do now?

2
More Problems

Jesse raced to the library corner. Maybe he could find a book he could read in a hurry. One with few words and lots of pictures. But all those books had been taken. He searched for something, anything.

"Jesse," Ms. Noori called. "We're waiting."

Quickly he grabbed a book with an old man on the cover. Its title was *The Hero of* ———. He didn't know the last word.

Maybe the old man was a president—George Washington or Abe Lincoln. He knew a little about Abe and George. But was the man on the cover one of them? He couldn't remember what they looked like, not exactly anyway.

Jesse hopped over to the reading group. Everyone else sat in the circle.

"Jesse's *always* last," Lyddie said. "And why does he always hop?" She made little fists with her hands and pressed them into her sides.

Jesse glared at her as he fell into the chair between Bip and Will. They always saved a place for him, no matter how late he was.

While Ms. Noori was writing on the chalkboard, Jesse showed Bip the cover of his book. "Abe Lincoln?" he whispered.

Bip shook his head.

"Washington?" Jesse tried.

Bip nodded.

One by one each Super Turtle gave a book report. They told the title and the author, what the book was about, and what they liked best. Sometimes Ms. Noori asked if they had a favorite part they wanted to read out loud.

11

Jesse looked at his book and swallowed. His mouth felt dry. What did he know about Washington? He flipped through the pages. What if Ms. Noori asked him to read? Would he stumble all over the words?

"Jesse, it's your turn," Ms. Noori said.

Uh-oh! Jesse gulped. What if Bip was wrong? What if the man wasn't George Washington?

"Um . . . I . . . ah . . . I lost my first tooth! And my dad's trading me a shark's tooth for it!" he said. He grinned widely and pointed to the space where his tooth had been. Jesse was sure the Super Turtles would be impressed. A real-life report was better than a book report.

"That's wonderful, Jesse," Ms. Noori said. "But teeth aren't going to get us to the police

station. Book reports are. Now please give us your report."

He wiggled in his chair. Wow, it felt uncomfortable. He stuck the tip of his tongue into the hole where his tooth had been. It didn't feel quite as wonderful as before. "Ah, I can't give my report. Ah . . . I can't find my book. This isn't the one I read." That was almost the truth.

The way Ms. Noori sat staring at him, he wondered if she could see inside his brain, read his thoughts. Teachers could do that, he'd heard. *Uh-oh.* "But I'll have three by Friday, I promise. Will you put my name on the Lost Tooth Chart now?" He glanced at Bip and Will and smiled.

"I'd rather put your name on the Book Report Chart, Jesse. But yes, I'll put your name on the tooth chart. Give me your tooth, and I'll keep it for you until after school."

Jesse hurried back to his desk. A crumpled wad of paper rested on top of Hernando. His tooth was gone!

3
The Tooth Gremlin

Jesse uncrumpled the note.

```
Thanks for the super,
spectacular, sensational
tooth.
                The Tooth Gremlin
```

Jesse showed Ms. Noori the note, and she read it out loud. "Oh, dear," she said. "Tooth Gremlin, indeed!"

15

Ms. Noori took the tooth box from her desk and set it on a table at the front of the room. "Now, I want each of you to pretend to get Jesse's tooth out of your desks," she said to all the kids. "Then come up here and pretend to put the tooth in the box."

Jesse thought Ms. Noori was pretty smart. The Tooth Gremlin would put the tooth in the box if he or she could do it secretly. Maybe.

Every kid walked up to the box and pretended to put a tooth in, even Bip and Will.

"This is dumb," complained Lyddie.

"Clever," said Maxine, walking right behind her.

16

Zach didn't say anything as he filed by Jesse's desk. But Jesse noticed his right hand was curled around something. Was it Zach who had taken Jesse's tooth?

After every kid had pretended to put a tooth in the box, Ms. Noori opened it. Empty!

Jesse swallowed. Now what? Right at this very moment his dad was probably in man-to-shark combat, risking his life to get a tooth just for him. And Jesse couldn't even hang on to one little baby tooth. He had to get that tooth back—no matter what.

At recess, Jesse questioned every kid in Blue Unit.

"I wouldn't touch your slimy old tooth. Yuk!" Alexandra told him.

"I have all the teeth I need," said Chad, the class collector of weird things.

"Hey, I'm your buddy," said Zach. "Why would I steal your tooth?"

"Well, somebody did!" Jesse said.

"Well, it wasn't me!" Zach said, and stomped off.

18

As Jesse plopped into an empty swing to puzzle things out, he felt a tap-tap on his shoulder.

"I'll help you find the thief," a voice behind him said.

4
To Catch a Thief

Jesse turned around to see Maxine smiling at him. Two new teeth with jagged edges poked through her pink gums.

"You?" Jesse said. Everyone knew that Maxine's goal in life was to be a detective. And she was smart. Everybody knew that, too. Maybe she *could* help him find the thief. "All right."

Maxine pushed up her sleeves and

rubbed her hands together. "OK, what sort of evidence do you have?"

Jesse yanked the note from his pocket.

"Tooth Gremlin. Hmm, very interesting," Maxine said, pulling on an earlobe.

As Jesse sat in the swing watching Maxine pull on her earlobe, he remembered she did weird things sometimes. Twice she had called him on the phone to see if he'd done his homework. Once she had chewed him out for not wearing his bike helmet.

Maxine unzipped her backpack. "Tell you what I think." She snatched a small black notebook, a green-glow pencil, and a book. "We need to do research. Read *The Clues in the Cluttered Closet* and report back tomorrow."

Jesse drummed his fingertips on the top

21

of his blue-and-orange Knicks cap. "*The Clues in the Cluttered Closet*?"

"Yep," Maxine said. "It may give you some ideas where to start."

The telephone was ringing as Jesse walked in the door from school that afternoon.

"You'd better not keep us from going to

the police station," a muffled voice whispered. "It would be a crime!" *Click.* The dial tone hummed in Jesse's ear.

"Who was that?" asked Auntie Lou.

"Wrong number," Jesse said. He didn't want to worry his aunt. After all, she had driven all the way from Oshkosh to stay with him. She had stayed with him two other times when his parents were away. His mom wrote travel books. Sometimes his dad went along. "To help carry the suitcases," his mom said. Dad was very strong, and Mom had lots of suitcases.

Almost as soon as Jesse hung up, the phone rang again.

"Wrong number!" he shouted into the receiver.

"Jesse?" *Uh-oh*, it was his dad!

"Dad! Hi!"

"What's with this 'wrong number'?" Dad asked.

"Oh, I thought you were someone playing a trick. Did you get the shark's tooth?"

"Not yet. But I've got a couple more days.

24

Lost your tooth yet?"

Jesse stuck the tip of his tongue into the tooth hole. "It came out today." Jesse couldn't tell his dad that he had *really* lost it. Maybe he would change his mind about getting the shark's tooth.

"That's super, Jesse! Hold on to it, and Saturday we'll make that trade. Now Mom wants to talk to you."

"Hi, Jesse," Mom said. Her voice made his eyes water, but it was his nose that started dripping. "How's school?"

"Good. We're going to the police station."

"Why? Did someone commit a crime?" His mom was always making jokes.

Should he tell her someone really had committed a crime? Someone had taken his tooth, snatched it right out from under Hernando Hernandez's nose?

"Mom, I . . . ah . . . I lost my tooth."

"All right!" his mom shouted into the phone. "That's wonderful. I can't wait to see you! I probably won't recognize you, you'll look so grown-up. I love you, Jesse."

"I love you, too."

Jesse wiped his nose with the back of his hand and gave the phone to his aunt. He had to get his tooth back. He just had to.

5
Don't Let the Bedbugs Bite!

After Auntie Lou hung up the phone, Jesse showed her the empty space in his mouth, but he didn't tell her about the empty feeling in his stomach.

"You're growing up, Jesse. It's a sign," she said.

Then he told her what happened to the tooth and showed her the note.

"Well, whoever the Tooth Gremlin is, he

or she is sure a good speller. *Spectacular* and *sensational* are hard words! But I'm sure you'll figure out who the Tooth Gremlin is and get your tooth back before Saturday." She mussed up his hair. "Want to help me bake chocolate chip cookies? You can read me the recipe."

While the cookies were baking, he went next door to Bip's house. They played basketball.

After supper, the phone rang. "Have you read the book yet?" This time he knew who the caller was. Maxine.

"What book?"

"*The Clues in the Cluttered Closet!*"

Jesse hung up the phone. Maxine was off her noodle. What could a book tell him about finding his tooth? He turned on his favorite TV show.

At nine o'clock Auntie Lou said, "Time for bed."

When Jesse went into the bathroom to brush his teeth, he looked into the mirror. The empty spot in his mouth made him feel happy *and* sad. Maybe he would never get his tooth back. What would he tell his dad? Would he give him the shark's tooth anyway?

Then he remembered—*The Clues in the Cluttered Closet*. Well, what could it hurt? he thought. But where was it? He didn't even remember bringing it home! All he could remember was Maxine handing it to him on the playground. After that Bip and Will had asked him to play basketball.

Jesse decided to check his backpack, even though he knew it wasn't there.

The backpack was stuffed with scrunched-up papers, pencil stubs, gum wrappers, a couple of baseball cards, and a book—*The Clues in the Cluttered Closet*! Weird. He didn't remember putting it there.

"Hop into bed," Auntie Lou said at his bedroom door.

The book still in his hand, he jumped into bed and pulled the covers over him.

"Sleep tight. Don't let the bedbugs bite," she said. She pulled the covers down and kissed him on the cheek. "Remember your prayers."

He wished he had remembered not to breathe. Auntie Lou smelled just like Mom, and that made him think of her. Then he thought of Dad, and all that thinking made his eyes water and his nose drip. He was glad when Auntie Lou turned out the light. He wiped his eyes and nose on the sheet and tried to think of a prayer. "Dear God. Help me find my tooth. Amen," he whispered.

Jesse stared up. He could see nothing in the dark, not even the ceiling. But God could see everything. Even Jesse's tooth. If only He would tell him where it was!

Jesse heard a voice inside his head. But it wasn't God's voice, it was a girl's. Maxine's. *"The Clues in the Cluttered Closet,"* her voice seemed to whisper.

Jesse rolled out of bed and tiptoed to his dresser. He kept a flashlight in his top drawer, for emergencies. After his fingers found it, he crawled back under the covers, flipped on the light, and began reading. *Sly heard footsteps behind him. He didn't dare turn around. He knew who was following him—Shadow!* Jesse didn't put the book down until he had finished it. Sly had solved the case and had given Jesse an idea how to solve his own. He couldn't wait for the next day!

6
Clues

The next morning Jesse met Maxine on the playground. She was waiting for him by the swings.

Maxine whipped out her notebook and the green-glow pencil. "So, what'd you find out?"

"Clues. We need to list all the *clues*." He was surprised Maxine hadn't thought of that. Maybe she was smart, but she had a lot to learn about being a detective. Sly knew the importance of clues. Jesse had learned that last night under the covers.

"All right, go," Maxine said.

"Clue number one," Jesse began. "The note was written on a computer." Jesse waited as Maxine wrote clue number one in her notebook. "Clue number two," Jesse continued. "The thief used big words." Maxine wrote clue number two in her notebook. "Clue number three," Jesse said. "The words were spelled right." Maxine wrote down clue number three, then snapped her notebook shut.

"Good start," she said, "but clues aren't enough. It's going to take a little more research. Read *The Crazy Crocodile Caper* and meet me before school tomorrow." Maxine reached into her backpack and pulled out *The Crazy Crocodile Caper*, a thick book with small print. Did she really expect him to read *that*?

At reading group that morning, Ms. Noori asked for his book report.

"Ah . . . ah . . . ," Jesse stammered. He had been thinking so hard about clues, he had forgotten all about book reports.

"Jesse will *never* have a book report," Lyddie said. "He's going to keep the whole unit from going to the police station. It's not fair!"

Then Jesse remembered. *The Clues in the Cluttered Closet*! He told the Super Turtles all about it. "And tomorrow you'll hear about this." He showed them *The Crazy Crocodile Caper*.

"You can't read that," Lyddie said. "It's got too many words!"

Maybe Lyddie was right. It *was* a thick book.

As soon as Jesse got home, Auntie Lou asked, "Any luck finding the Tooth Gremlin?"

Jesse shook his head.

"Well, don't give up," she said. "You'll figure something out before your mom and dad get back."

"I've got to. Dad's bringing a shark's tooth for it. And those are hard to get."

Auntie Lou mussed up his hair again. Good thing he didn't care much about combing it anyway.

37

After chocolate chip cookies and a glass of milk, Jesse went to his bedroom to read *The Crazy Crocodile Caper*. Lyddie was right. The book was too hard for him. He didn't know half of the words. What was Maxine thinking? Not very much for someone so smart.

Jesse brought the book to Auntie Lou, who sat reading the paper in his dad's big leather chair. "Do you like mysteries?"

"Sure."

"Want to help me read this one?"

"You bet I do."

Jesse crawled into the chair with his aunt.

By the time Jesse reached the final chapter, Auntie Lou had to flick on a light. It was such a good book, Jesse forgot why he was reading it until he turned the last page and

Auntie Lou said, "There sure were a lot of suspects, weren't there?"

"Yeah. Detective Tracy was pretty smart to figure out the thief was Mirabelle," Jesse said.

"She sure had me fooled!"

"I bet Detective Tracy could find the Tooth Gremlin," Jesse said.

"I bet *you* can, too," Auntie Lou said. She ruffled his hair, of course.

Jesse thought about what Auntie Lou had just said.

"You're right! Detective Tracy gave me a great idea!"

Tomorrow he would tell Maxine what that idea was.

7
Suspects

"Suspects," Jesse told Maxine Wednesday morning. "We make a list of *suspects*." The word sent a ripple of excitement down Jesse's spine. He was getting closer to finding his tooth. He felt it in his bones.

"OK, go," Maxine said, whipping out the notebook and the green-glow pencil again.

"Whoever wrote the note has a computer," Jesse said. He thought for a moment.

"No, whoever wrote the note *used* a computer."

He ran to the computer lab.

Maxine followed him.

A schedule was posted next to the door.

"Maxine, write this down—Chad Dunlop, Zachary Montbriand, Alexandra Whitney, and Maxine Macmillan had computer lab from nine-thirty to ten o'clock, the time the tooth was stolen and replaced with the note!"

Maxine recorded the suspects in her notebook, then snapped it shut. "We're getting closer." Maxine pulled out another book and thrust it at Jesse. "Read this, then meet me on the playground after school."

Jesse stared at the title. *The Mystery of the Missing Mummy*? What could a missing mummy tell him about finding his missing tooth? Well, he had learned something in the other two books, so maybe he could learn something in this one, also.

When Jesse hopped into class, he saw Ms. Noori putting *The Clues in the Cluttered Closet* next to his name on the Book Report Chart. It made him smile. He stuck the tip of his tongue into his tooth hole. If only he had his tooth, everything would be perfect!

In reading group, he gave his report on *The Crazy Crocodile Caper*. Lyddie's eyes nearly popped out of her head. Then he said, "I've got clues and suspects for my missing tooth. I'm about to crack the case." And he looked right at Lyddie, who looked away. Of course! Why had he forgotten about Lyddie?

She was a suspect, too! When he got back to his desk, he would add her name to the list.

At his desk, he wrote LYDDIE on a piece of paper. But something wasn't quite right. Even though Lyddie was a prime suspect, how could she have taken his tooth? She was in his reading group when the crime took place.

Jesse stared at Lyddie and scratched his head. Then he looked at Chad, Zach, Alexandra, and Maxine and scratched it again. Maybe *The Mystery of the Missing Mummy* would give him some new ideas. He was close, but not close enough, and he had to get the tooth back soon. He only had two more days.

Jesse pulled the book out of his desk. He read it every free moment he had. When Ms. Noori finally said, "It's time to go home," Jesse turned the last page. Did he have something to tell Maxine! Something big!

8
Putting Two and Two Together

After school, Maxine waited for Jesse on the playground. Jesse ran up to her. "We need to compare the thief with the suspects! Write this down, Max."

THE THIEF

1 Had computer lab between nine-thirty and ten o'clock on Monday.

2. Uses big words.

3. Is a good speller.

47

THE SUSPECTS

1. Chad Dunlop—not a good speller; doesn't use big words.
2. Alexandra Whitney—not a good speller; uses big words.
3 & 4. Zachary Montbriand and Maxine Macmillan—both good spellers. Both use very big words.

Maxine pulled on an earlobe. "Hmm. But the lab's writing program has a spell check."

"Oh no," Jesse moaned. He flopped down on the ground. "That means even a bad speller could have written that note!"

"Here. This might help." Maxine handed Jesse *The Diary of the Dizzy Detective.* "Tomorrow before school, meet me here."

Dizzy detective? Jesse felt dizzy all right. Would one more book really help him find the thief and get his tooth back? His mom and dad would be home in two more days. He just had to get that tooth!

On his way home, Jesse started reading *The Diary of the Dizzy Detective*. He'd never walked and read a book before. It made him

dizzy—clues, suspects, and now one more thing, the same thing that had made the detective in the story so dizzy!

"Motives," Jesse told Maxine the next morning. "We need to look for *motives*."

Maxine started pulling on her earlobe so hard, Jesse thought she might yank it out.

"Motives are what had made the detective so dizzy," he told Maxine. "None of the suspects in *The Diary of the Dizzy Detective* had a good motive." Jesse thought about his own suspects. "Chad collects weird things," he said. "Zach's mad at me for suspecting him. . . . Alexandra would never *touch* a tooth. . . . And you . . . you're trying to help me." Jesse scratched his head and thought very hard.

50

Why would someone steal his tooth? Why would they want it? Jesse stuck his tongue in his tooth hole. Or . . . maybe they didn't want it. Maybe someone was just playing a trick on him.

But who?

And why?

What was the motive?

Motive. The word triggered a string of thoughts inside Jesse's brain.

Motive . . . police station . . . Detective Kelly . . . one hundred book reports . . .

Jesse stared at Maxine. "You! You did it! You made me read books. You'd do anything to get to the police station. Even commit a crime!"

Maxine stopped pulling on her earlobe

51

and started to smile. She handed Jesse another book, *The Mystery of the Secret Friends*.

"Open it up," she said.

Jesse opened the book and found a special compartment inside. In it rested Jesse's tooth.

By recess that morning, Jesse had four books next to his name on the Book Report Chart and one tooth on the Lost Tooth Chart.

After recess, Ms. Noori said, "We have one hundred and one book reports. Tomorrow we will *all* visit Detective Kelly at the police station."

Everyone clapped, even Lyddie.

Jesse looked over at Maxine. She was looking at the Book Report Chart. This time she was smiling. Maxine did some weird things, but she sure was smart. *Four books in*

one week! Jesse almost laughed out loud. But wait until tomorrow. Wait until Detective Kelly heard about the case of the missing tooth *he* solved—and the shark's tooth it was going to earn him!

What a Mouthful!

Don't be puzzled! Be a puzzle solver like Jesse and have fun solving the ones below.

Too Many Tooths!

Jesse's tooth is missing, but in this puzzle there are lots of them. The word *TOOTH* is hidden in this word search ten times. The words go up, down, backward, sideways, and diagonally. Circle the words when you find them.

```
T O O T H S M P T T
S H T O A T I H O M
R T O O Z O H T T Z
H O O T O S H O O H
O O T H X T L O O T
F T H S M O H T T O
T X T O O T H X H O
Z R I T O O T H X T
```

The Tooth Exchange

Jesse was eager to trade his own tooth for a tooth that belongs to one of these. Color all the spaces that equal six and you'll find the answer to this question.

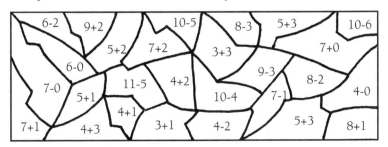

Cracking the Case

There are three types of lists Jesse made to help him solve the case of his missing tooth. To find out what they are, cross out the letters X, Y, and Z. Write the letters that are left in the spaces to the right.

CXLZUYES — *clues*

XSUZSPEXCTYS — *suspects*

XZMOZYTIXVEYS — *motives*

Turtle Time

Jesse's reading group is called Super Turtles. Below are five turtles. Circle the turtle that is different from the rest to find the real Super Turtle.

A   B   C   D   E

Solving the Mystery

With help from Maxine, Jesse solved the mystery of his missing tooth! What could he now be called? To find the answer, follow the code. Write the letters in the spaces below.

E= ☀ H= ♡ L= 🐟 O= 🪰 S= ☆ T= 🦋 U= 🎧

T O O t h *s l e u t h*
🦋 🪰 🪰 🦋 ♡   ☆ 🐟 ☀ 🎧 🦋 ♡

From Here to There

The Kids in Ms. Noori's class were trying to earn a trip to the local police station. Follow the maze and get the kids from the school to the station.

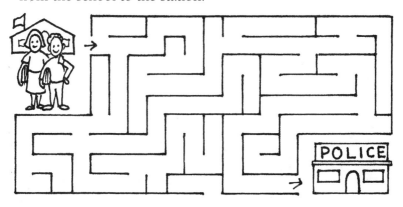

Look For Books

Jesse ended up reading several books. Ms. Noori and his classmates were very impressed! Impress yourself—find and circle the nine hidden books in the picture below.

Puzzle Answers

Too Many Tooths

Cracking the Case

CLUES
SUSPECTS
MOTIVES

Solving the Mystery

Tooth Sleuth

The Tooth Exchange

Turtle Time

Turtle D is different.

From Here to There

POLICE

Look for Books